Room 23 and the Lock-Down Drill

SUNSHINE ELEMENTARY SCHOOL

Suzanne Wolf and Guy Grace

Illustrated by Michelle Nethercot

AuthorHouse™
1663 Liberty Drive
Bloomington, IN 47403
www.authorhouse.com
Phone: 1 (800) 839-8640

Published by AuthorHouse 10/01/2018

Library of Congress Control Number: 2018911627

ISBN: 978-1-5462-6139-1 (sc)
ISBN: 978-1-5462-6140-7 (e)

authorHOUSE®

Dedicated to my beloved mother, Angela. I miss you deeply every day and keep you alive and present in all that I do. You always signed all of your notes to me this way so I will do the same here: "I love, adore, and cherish you! XOXO"

It was another beautiful day at Sunshine Elementary School. Miss Kindheart couldn't wait to pick up her students to begin their exciting new learning adventures of the day. Safety Squirrel, the school mascot, was always close behind making sure everyone was doing the right thing at the right time.

Once she collected all of the excited students from the playground and they walked quietly through the hallway to their room, she said, "Good morning, Room 23!" "GOOD MORNING MISS KINDHEART!" the class boomed out at the same time.

"Let's please quickly get to our morning routines with attendance and lunch count."

All of a sudden, a booming announcement came through the loud speaker. *Everyone* was startled!

Normally they knew exactly what to do during their morning routines, but this announcement was something different.

It said,

"Lock down! Lock down! Lock down! Alert others, shelter and lock the classroom doors! Lights out! Stay quiet and out of the hallway line of sight! If you are unable to get to a secure location, hide or flee immediately to the nearest safe location away from the school! If you are outside, alert others, and flee away from the school to the nearest safe location."

The students were confused. They started scrambling around, bumping into each other. A few of the students started to cry.

Miss Kindheart clapped her hands very loudly and with intention—it was the "clap, clap, clap-clap-clap" signal that meant "All eyes on me and mouths closed tightly."

The students immediately stopped, became silent, and all eyes were trained on Miss Kindheart.

"Class, I will explain later. Right now, I need everyone to go quietly into the corner by the backpacks and sit crisscross applesauce."

The students did exactly as they were told. Zoë sat by one of the scared girls, holding her hand and helping her not to cry. The other students held hands and bravely sat without making a peep.

Miss Kindheart quickly locked the door and covered the small window with a prepared piece of construction paper. Then she went over to the windows and closed the blinds.

She whispered, "Room 23, I am proud of how quickly and quietly you followed directions. I will answer questions later. The first thing you need to know is someone is going to try opening the door—pretty hard. This is scary, but this will be someone in our building making sure our door is locked and no one can get in."

"For right now, we're just going to sit quietly. I want you to trust me and to know that the most important job I have is to keep you safe."

Sure enough, it wasn't long before the door handle started shaking and rattling loudly. Some of the students gasped, trying to stay quiet. The students were relieved to hear the strong voice of Mr. Kelly, their principal, "Room 23 is locked tightly."

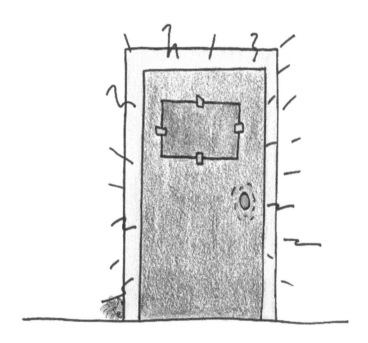

Eventually, another announcement came over the loud speaker. It was Mr. Kelly again. "Sunshine Elementary, thank you for being so cooperative and helpful. The morning announcement was actually a drill. Boys and Girls, your teachers will spend time with you answering some questions. You may resume your regular classroom activities. Have a great day of learning!"

Everyone in the school must have given a huge sigh of relief at the same time because it felt like the whole building sighed right along with them!

Suddenly, there was a knock at the door. Miss Kindheart took the construction paper off the window and looked to see who was there through the window. "Class, our good friend, Officer Michael, is at the door! He must be here to explain what just happened."

Miss Kindheart went to open the door but it wouldn't open. She giggled a little bit. "Oops! I forgot to unlock the door!" Miss Kindheart could be forgetful sometimes.

She welcomed Officer Michael who said as he entered the room, "Thank you Miss Kindheart, and goooood morning Room 23!" in his warm, powerful voice.

"Hello Officer Michael!" the class sang in unison. They loved it when the head security officer came to visit them. It made them feel so special.

"Boys and Girls," he continued, "I am so proud of Miss Kindheart! She locked her door tightly, and I couldn't get in. That was precisely what she needed to do."

"But I also want you to know that I have a key to this room. NEVER open the door for someone during a lock-down alert, even if they say they're the police, your principal, or anyone else. I'm one of the safe people who has permission to open this door and all the doors in the building. In a lock-down situation, you never need to open it for me – or for anyone."

"Thank you, Officer Michael!" the students chimed up automatically.

"Room 23, Officer Michael is here to teach you about our new safety routine, and he then will answer questions when he is done. Otherwise, you know what will happen...."

The students giggled, and Alex said, "Yep, we'll be talkin' for days!"

Officer Michael had to let out a big hearty chuckle. "Thank you for keeping me on track, Alex!"

"Now, what did you notice this morning when you heard the announcement?"

Immediately hands popped up. "Mason?" Miss Kindheart asked.

Mason started to mumble nervously, "`Err... ahh... we had to go sit quietly in the corner by the backpacks."

"Good," Officer Michael affirmed while walking toward the door. "There's a reason why you had to go to that corner." He took off the construction paper covering the window, stepped outside, closed the door, and then looked back in through the window.

The children wondered what he was doing, especially because he kept looking around.

He came back into the room and said, "When I was looking around, I could only see a very small part of the classroom—this included you all in the Learning Circle."

"Oh, I get it!" Sumiko said, "You can't see over in the corner."

"Yes," Officer Michael smiled. "This is going to become part of your safety routine when you hear the announcement for a lock down."

"Lock-down drill?!" Jacy shouted out before he could remember to raise his hand. "Don't we only do *fire* drills?"

"Well, that is a great question, Jacy." "How many of you remember practicing for a fire drill?"

Everyone's hand shot up.

Miss Kindheart continued, "Excellent. Now, does anyone know how many fires we've had at Sunshine Elementary?"

Cambria slowly raised her hand. She wasn't sure of the answer, but she was brave enough to try anyway, "I don't think we've ever had any."

Miss Kindheart smiled and said, "That's correct, Cambria!"

Alex blurted out, "Wow, we've never had a fire?! So why do we keep practicing?"

Miss Kindheart calmly responded, "Students, no one ever *wants* a fire to happen, but we plan on how to stay safe if there is one, just in case."

Officer Michael agreed. "Yes, Room 23, fires hardly ever happen. The same goes for a lock-down situation, but we always want to be prepared!"

"That's right! Like any safety routine we have put in place, you practice it over and over, so in case something does happen, then you spring into action! And you feel confident about what you need to do."

Officer Michael continued, "First of all, let's talk about how our school is already safe in so many ways: The outside doors are locked, and you have to buzz to get in. There are cameras everywhere, and there are people that work for me that are always watching what's going on around your school."

"Like when my mom and I had to press the buzzer to get into the school this morning? Her car wouldn't start so we were a bit late." Reyna explained.

Officer Michael said, "That's right, Reyna. We've worked very hard in the security department to make sure we always know who is at the school and why they are there."

"First, let's talk about why the school goes into lock down. If my security team (or someone working in the school) notices something or someone on the camera that they feel makes it unsafe for you, someone in the office is notified immediately, and the school becomes locked. No one can get into the school."

Room 23 got very quiet, still, and their eyes all grew as large as saucers.

Officer Michael continued, "I know that sounds scary, but remember, it doesn't hardly ever happen."

Stevie raised his hand nervously and asked, "Was there a bad guy at our school this morning?"

Officer Michael kept his kind eyes on the whole group and softly replied, "No there wasn't anyone unsafe in the building. But I will give you an example of a real lock-down situation at another school just last week."

"My security department was busy doing their job, and they noticed someone walking around the school that seemed confused."

"It was around lunch and recess time. This person was walking back and forth around the edge of the playground, and they were holding what looked like a case that could hold a gun."

"We weren't sure what it was, and because your safety is most important, we called the police and then announced the lock-down alert. So while you were hiding safely, the police were on their way."

"Was it a bad guy with a gun?" Coral asked, in a scared voice.

"Thankfully, no. It was an empty case, and everything was fine." Officer Michael reassured them.

"Oh," exclaimed Anthony, "That's like when I forgot my toy car in my pocket and the security buzzer went off at the airport. They had to make sure I wasn't carrying anything unsafe."

"Exactly!" smiled Officer Michael proudly. "We check everything that looks like something that is possibly harmful. Almost always, it's nothing. But we must check anyway, just to be sure."

Officer Michael looked at the class and said, "I want you to know why I am already proud of you before you learn anymore about this new routine."

"You and your teacher already knew instinctively how to stay safe before ever learning these rules! You are going to be even better at it once I explain the rest of the routine, and you practice it."

Officer Michael discussed the important points to remember in this new safety routine: "Okay Class, the first thing that happens is you will hear an announcement over the loudspeaker like you did this morning."

"When a lock down is announced in your school, you need to do three basic things: first, find a safe place that is out of the way of danger."

Jaden piped up, "Like in the corner away from the window in the door."

"Yes!" Officer Michael said. "The next thing to do is **stay** out of danger. This means to stay very quiet and in one place."

"Then, you all need to make sure that everyone else is staying quiet and calm, and you are doing what you are supposed to do, just like you practiced today."

Reyna said, "Like when Zoë held my hand and helped calm me down."

Officer Michael was beaming and said, "Okay Rock Stars, tell me what else you need to do."

Everyone raised their hands. Miss Kindheart called on Zoë. "Miss Kindheart, you locked the door and put that construction paper on the window."

"And she also went over and closed the blinds," Josiah chimed in.

Officer Michael clapped his hands. "You guys are awesome! But there's one more important thing that you all didn't do."

When you're in a lock down, it's important to sit in a position that will allow you to spring into action."

"You need to sit crisscross applesauce but be ready to jump up quickly."

"Let's practice that action!" Officer Michael said enthusiastically.

Micah bounced right up from where he was sitting and started boinging up and down. The rest of the class joined in quickly and had fun popping up and down like jumping beans from where they were sitting.

Miss Kindheart allowed them a few minutes of fun since they had been sitting so nicely for a while. When she clapped her signal, they all quieted down.

Just then, Mr. Kelly knocked on the door. That made the kids jump a little—they were still a bit unnerved by what had happened that day.

The kind principal walked in with Dimitri who had been at the dentist that morning and missed the drill and discussion.

Dimitri said as he came into the room, "Miss Kindheart, I'm sorry I'm late, but as I was on my way to the classroom, I heard an announcement, and the 1st grade teacher grabbed me and had me sit in her classroom back in the corner. What happened?"

"Dimitri," Officer Michael said, "that must have felt confusing and a bit scary. We have been talking about what it means when the school goes into a lock down."

"Now Class, let's go over what the rule is if you are in the hallway. If there is a teacher pulling you into their classroom, it's okay."

"Dimitri, if that first-grade teacher hadn't pulled you into her classroom, the next option for you would have been to find an empty room, lock the door, and hide in there until you hear the announcement that the lock-down drill is over."

HALL OR OFFICE

- GO TO THE FIRST UNLOCKED CLASSROOM AND HIDE
- IF AN ADULT IS THERE - FOLLOW THEIR DIRECTIONS ON WHERE TO HIDE
- IF YOU ARE ALONE:
  - LOCK THE DOOR
  - FIND THE BEST HIDING PLACE
- AN ADULT FROM YOUR SCHOOL WILL BE LOOKING FOR YOU!
- GO BACK TO YOUR CLASSROOM WHEN THE LOCKDOWN IS OVER
- WAIT AS PATIENTLY AS YOU CAN -- HELP IS ON THE WAY!

Officer Michael looked around at all the students. "It's the only time you have permission to be in a classroom without an adult."

"Officer Michael, we just discussed a couple of possibilities of having students out of the classroom. Can we please go through some other scenarios of what to do if a student is **not** in the classroom with their teacher?" Miss Kindheart asked. "What if you are in the bathroom?" a few students were heard whispering.

Officer Michael reached for his poster for the bathroom. "It is very important to know about the safety routine in the bathroom!"

If you are in the bathroom during a lock-down drill: stay inside of the bathroom stall, lock the door, stand up carefully on the toilet, and then crouch down to stay hidden as best you can.

Officer Michael had one more important detail to go over about staying safe during a lock-down event. "Boys and Girls, it might be possible that while you are in a lock down, that the fire alarm goes off. That might seem confusing about which safety routine to put into action, so let me help give you some guidelines for this situation."

If you are already in lock down and the fire alarm goes off, you must use your senses! Smell for smoke and look for fire. If there is no evidence of a fire – stay put and continue your safety routine for lock downs!

But if you do smell smoke or see evidence of fire, you must leave the building just like your fire safety routine.

"Remember, Room 23" Miss Kindheart added, "The chances of this happening are SO tiny (and she showed them with her fingers close together), that we are just learning what to do so we can feel confident about how to stay safe."

Officer Michael agreed. "One last important detail to go over in our new safety routine, is what to do if you are not in your classroom and all the doors are locked. This is when you also have permission to run outside."

"We get to run out of the building?" several kids shrieked. Miss Kindheart reminded them to be attentive listeners – especially for this part.

Officer Michael repeated, "Room 23, it is important to think of all the places you might end up being when the lock-down alert goes off. If you are not in your classroom, the bathroom, or another classroom, you might find that all of the doors are locked. We need you to know that it is during that time that you have permission to go outside and hide."

"I have an idea!" smiled Officer Michael. "Let's go practice the best way to hide outside together. I always learn better by practicing the right way!"

Room 23 lined up anxiously to learn the right way to hide outside.

They all followed Officer Michael outside to see where to hide **only if all the nearby doors were locked.** Officer Michael had several students demonstrate how to hide behind certain bushes. He also showed them some spots on the playground behind trees.

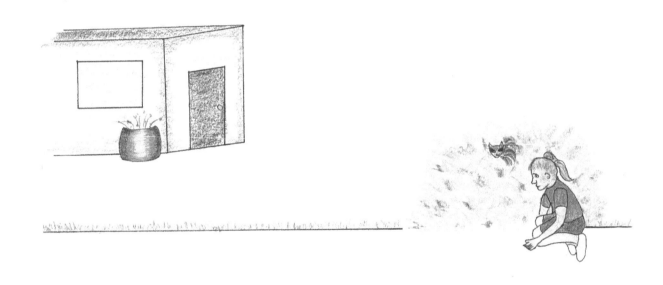

This was the one time that playing Hide and Seek was for **safety** and Room 23 understood the difference.

"Room 23! You have done a fantastic job learning a new safety routine today!" Officer Michael said proudly. "I am sure you might have some questions and thoughts you'd like to share, and I want you to make a list with Miss Kindheart so I can come back and answer them!"

"For now, though, I think it's time to play!" Miss Kindheart announced. "Let's thank Officer Michael so much for teaching us today!" I know he needs to go to another school to teach more kids this new safety routine!

"THANK YOU, OFFICER MICHAEL!!!!" Room 23 sang loudly together.

They each gave him a high five. Miss Kindheart reminded all of them that now was the time to play Hide and Seek for fun!

All of Room 23 scampered around the places that were in bounds on the playground. "I'll be IT!" shouted Alex.

Everyone was glad that they knew what to do if a lock-down alert happened. They knew they would have to practice it again, and that was okay in everyone's mind.

But they were even happier that it was time to get back to enjoying the day at Sunshine Elementary School!

And...Safety Squirrel? He was so excited about everyone learning all the ways to stay safe, that he decided to come out of hiding to show just how proud he was!

CPSIA information can be obtained
at www.ICGtesting.com
Printed in the USA
LVHW070109221218
601286LV00003B/15/P

9 781546 261391